The Fourth Wife

HE STILL AIN'T GET IT RIGHT

A MEMOIR BY

MEME WILLIAMS

To request permissions, contact the publisher at info@enterpromedia.com

Paperback: 978-0-578-71183-6

First paperback edition May 2020

Edited by Brinkley Fuller
Cover art by Brinkley Fuller
Layout by Brinkley Fuller
Photographs provided by MeMe Williams

Printed by Enterpromedia in the USA.

Enterpromedia
Birmingham, AL

www.enterpromedia.com

Dedication

I dedicate this book to my family and friends who have been there with me throughout this whole ordeal. I thank you for helping me in getting back to **ME!!** To everyone who is going through it, just know you can get out and be happy with the right person.

- *MeMe Williams*

The Beginning

Being a successful woman and staying on the grind is hard. Even with the ups and downs, I still make it work. I am the CEO and owner of DZIRE, Inc., a promotions and events company. I am also the owner of The Vault Bar and Lounge in Birmingham, Alabama.

I have tried dating for years and it has never worked well for me. After no luck in love, I focused on my businesses, family and friends. My business became more manageable and things were good with my family and close friends. I started to become open to being in a relationship and shifted my focus on dating someone. However, this almost caused me to lose it all and myself.

Here is my story…

I was at home scrolling through Facebook and I noticed this beautiful lake on this guy's page. His name was Chris and I messaged him and asked if it was located in Birmingham? He responded back and said, "It's in Huntsville, Alabama." After complimenting the view and brief conversation, we wished each other to have a good day.

On Christmas day, I received a message in my inbox from Chris asking about my day. After letting him know I didn't receive anything and ultimately my family was good and therefore I was also good. He asked for my email address and I assumed he was going to pitch me an idea or something random. To my surprised, I received a couple of emails from him for a massage and another one for dinner, for my family and I.

I was so overwhelmed with these surprises, because no one has ever done anything for me in that capacity and especially from a stranger. So, I offered drinks if he ever visited The Vault. He replied, "I don't want anything from you and I only wanted you to smile."

He asked, "If I worked at The Vault?" and I told him, I own it. A couple of days later, we met at the Botanical Gardens in Birmingham. It felt weird at first, because I don't typically do dating. Throughout my life, dating has not turned out good for me. So, I figured I give it a chance again.

As soon as he came out of his car and started walking towards me, I noticed he had a man purse and I was a bit confused like, 'What the hell?'. We greeted each other and started walking into the Gardens. We sat down and he opened his man purse and brought 2 mini bottles of wine, fruit, and cheese. I felt at ease and burst out laughing. I told him I thought he was a bit suspect due to his man purse.

We both laughed and had a great time. We were there until the lights were turned off. We talked for hours and during our conversation, I asked him, has he ever been married before and he said, "Yes, three times."

I know, I was looking like, what the hell?

He explained that he married his first wife in his late teens. Then, the second wife, he thought he had it right, but it didn't work out. The third wife, he mentioned they were together for a while. They took a trip to Vegas and got sloppy drunk and ended up at the chapel where they eloped. They quickly annulled the marriage when they got back home.

So, I thought...

At this point, I'm really enjoying the overall date and we went to dinner afterwards. He walked me to my car and proceeded to kiss me. I immediately stopped him and told him, "I don't know you like that!" I asked him, "Is this what everyone is doing now on the first date?" He said, "Yes and some go even further." I let him know that I don't get down like that. He respected that and hugged me and went to his hotel while I went home.

We started to get to know each other by talking and texting each other. The following week, I met him in Huntsville. He suggested I bring extra clothes in case I wanted to spend the night. I get to Huntsville and was thoroughly enjoying myself chilling watching TV.

The Fourth Wife

Next thing I know, he started kissing on my damn neck! He picked me up and took me to the bedroom and started kissing me all over.

He slowly caressed me and when his lips and tongue went in between my legs, it was a wrap and I was done!

He got me…

King of pussy and ass eater…

I was like shit… do you have a condom? He had me really good and we had a great weekend. He took me to the Botanical Gardens in Huntsville and I enjoyed the Butterfly Garden.

This was only the beginning…

Butterflies

February 2016

I was really digging him and we decided to start dating exclusively. One day, I flew to Newark to hang with my celebrity friend, who is more like a big brother. During our conversation, my brother told me, "Sis, something doesn't seem right about him, but if you really care about him, then I'm good."

I noticed Chris started acting suspicious around the celebrities and I confronted him about it. I asked him, "What's going on?" I reminded him that this is what I do for a living. I don't have a regular 9-5 job. I am the CEO of DZIRE, Inc. and I manage models and promote events.

Chris said he could handle my lifestyle, but his actions were totally different. Soon afterwards, I found out he recently fucked his ex-girlfriend. I confronted him about it and he had the audacity to tell me that he wanted to see if there were any feelings left for her and claimed his ex-girlfriend wanted to get back with him. Chris stated he didn't feel anything for her on that level and she had to leave.

Did I really believe that shit? Hell no!

The Fourth Wife

He proceeded to tell me that he did it, because he thought I was out of town cheating on him. I told Chris to be honest with me and let me know if he desired to see other people. He quickly apologized and said, "It was a mistake and I want to be with you."

At this point, I am beginning to get agitated with this man and he didn't fit my typical type of guy. His voice fucked me up at first, because it was very squeaky and I have never dated a slue-footed man either. One of my homegirl reminded me, "There is no perfect man" She said, "If he is treating you right, then let him in and enjoy yourself."

I pondered on what she said and began to think why I was falling in love with Chris. With Chris, I was able to relax and enjoy life more. I wasn't grinding so hard and I was able to slow down which I don't normally do.

In May, we decided to travel out of the country to Aruba and Curacao and I had the time of my life! While heading back to Aruba, Chris met with his fraternity brothers and I left the next day. So, I had some time to evaluate our relationship. I compared the good against the bad things in our lives and the good things outweighed the bad. I knew I was falling in love with him and just wanted to be around him all the time. So, when he got back from Aruba in June, we sat down a couple of weeks later to discuss our relationship. By June 2016, we decided to officially become a couple.

Chris began to start shit over simple things. He would tell me, "Delete your picture on Facebook, because your breasts are on him." It was non-stop verbal abuse and he was never satisfied. Plus, he was jealous about everything.

My sister and I went to Puerto Rico in August and were having a great time until Chris started acting a fool. He assumed I was wildin' out. I was really taken aback about it, because I thought we had an understanding. He decided to send me flowers through the hotel in an attempt to apologize.

Months go by and we are somewhat steady and I took him to California for his birthday. I knew how much he loved drinking wine and everything about it. I took him to an exclusive winery and resort where everything was simply beautiful.

Later, I found out one of his ex-girlfriends stayed in California and at this point I am getting pissed and now suspicious. He told me in the past that his ex-girlfriend was always cheating on him and never had time for him. He was communicating with her while we were on our California trip. I felt in my heart, he met with her too.

I started thinking about my last conversation with my brother. Ironically, he told me, "If Chris breaks your heart, we got problems." Unfortunately, I lost my brother a couple of weeks after that. I could not take it anymore and broke it off with Chris.

The Fourth Wife

After all of the bullshit, I went to Atlanta to hang with my friends for the One Music Festival. I was enjoying myself until I saw Chris with his fraternity brother and of course he wanted me to see him and I declined. The rest of the year was tumultuously with an on and off relationship.

Around the Christmas holidays, we went to Nashville, Tennessee with our kids. Things were really tensed, because we had a huge argument and by this point, I was over it. The verbal abuse continued with him calling me, "ghetto and ratchet" He really got pissed at me and started doing the most and petty shit. I didn't speak to him during the rest of the trip and I stayed in the room with my kids.

After Christmas, we talked and I mentioned to him, "let's make this work, because I'm tired of going back and forth." Chris told me he was going to think about it. Then, I mentioned the New Year was coming up and I have an upcoming surgery in January and let's bring it in with each other. To my surprised, he tells me he already made plans with his fraternity brother to visit his sister in Mississippi and to look at some land he might purchase.

I gave Chris an ultimatum to either move on or stay to make this relationship work, because I could not deal with the upcoming surgery and him. I told him; my body couldn't handle all of this stress. He assured me we were going to talk once he got back from his trip.

Ultimatum

January 2017

Chris drove straight to me from his trip on the night before my surgery. He was all over me and acted like he missed me and honestly, I missed him as well. I went down on him and we made love all night.

The next day, I had a hysterectomy and my right ovary removed due to blood clots. I was hospitalized for 3-4 days and I could not walk on my right leg for a while. Chris was there with me during this whole ordeal. He cooked, cleaned the house, and the whole nine yards. I fell back in love with him, because I was literally down and out. The fact that he was there for me was so unreal. Even when Chris went back to work, he checked on me every day to make sure I was good.

One day while recovering, I was resting in my bed scrolling through Facebook and something caught my attention. I found out Chris cheated on me with another woman during his Mississippi New Year trip. Y'all, I was sick to my stomach and even worse, I was still in pain from my surgery. I called him and asked, "Did you sleep with anyone while you were in Mississippi?" and he replied, "No."

I waited until he came back to Birmingham the following Thursday, since I knew he was staying over for the weekend. I confronted Chris face to face and asked him, "Did you sleep with someone during your trip in Mississippi?" and "it's best that you tell me the truth!" His ass still lied about the situation. I asked him, "Who is she?" At this point, he had a stupid look on his face. I said, "Did you fuck her and don't lie to me!". Chris replied, "Yes, but only one time, because she was annoying and talked too much" Y'all, I was so over this motherfucker! I told him, "Fool, you really expect me to believe you was with this woman for the whole weekend and fucked her once!"

"You really think I'm that stupid!"

"You are a nasty disgusting man!"

"You came straight to me and let me go down on you knowing you had been with this woman all weekend!"

We were already in my bedroom and I took some pain pills, because I was hurting so badly. I felt like I was losing my mind and I could not take it anymore! Back in December, I told Chris if this isn't what you want, then go ahead and move on. I was prepared to move on with my life and this selfish ass man pulled me back into this bullshit!

I locked myself in the bathroom and laid on the shower floor while the water was running. I cried my heart out. I crawled into my closet to console myself and he broke into the bathroom. He came into the closet and kept apologizing. By this time, the pain pills are beginning to settle in my system and all I could muster up to say, "Why did you do this to me?" I passed out due to the mental and physical stress with the addition of the pain pills.

Chris carried me to my bed after I passed out. I woke up and noticed he was still there and I really lost it!

"Get the hell out of my house!"

I went the fuck off and he kept apologizing. He told me he wasn't going anywhere, because he loved me.

"How in the hell can you fix your mouth to say that?"

"You don't love me; you love your own selfish self!"

"You don't think about no one, but you!"

Lord knows, if I had the strength, he would have received everything he deserved that day…

Chris sat in my bed and held me so tight, I could barely move. He then tells me, he was confused and scared to get back with me after what happened in Nashville. He was tired of arguing back and forth.

"Well, why the fuck did you come back here to me?"

He said, "I wasn't planning to get back with you. I

wanted to be there for you as I promised, because I knew you were scared of getting the surgery. When I came to your house on the day before the surgery and saw you, all of my feelings came back and I wanted to be with you again."

The pain intensified in my body, so I took more pain pills and passed out. I could not focus anymore, because my heart was broken all over again.

Y'all know I fell for the okie dokie again, right?

Two weeks later, my dumb ass let him back into my life! (I know, I know!).

Two in a half months later, I was able to walk again and my doctor cleared me to get out of the house. Chris took me to Chattanooga, because he knew I was going crazy in that house! We had a great time there and overall things were good.

We were getting along for a couple of months, but still having a few petty ass arguments until May. It was his annual Aruba trip with his fraternity brothers and I went to Jamaica with my sister. So, while I'm enjoying myself on my trip, he started picking arguments with me and accused me of messing around. I was not going to let him ruin my trip.

So, when we returned to the states, I stayed in Atlanta with my sister for a week. I did not want to go home or deal with seeing him, because I knew he was going to start arguing again. I came home to Birmingham for about a day and then drove to Huntsville to be with him. I greeted him and gave him the gift I bought in Jamaica. After he kissed me, we made love and chilled all night.

The next day, Chris went to work and I forgot my laptop. I asked if I could use his and he provided me his password. As soon I logged in, I went on Facebook to login to my account, but his page was already open.

Y'all…. You already know my ass went to his inbox.

Big *sigh*

Remember those annual Aruba trips?

Remember any trips with his fraternity brothers?

The shit I read and saw was so disgusting that I vomited. The fraternity brothers group he's apart of was beyond disgusting and I have plenty of evidence. Chris was talking to all kinds of women from in and out of the state. I literally blacked out and when I gathered myself, I got my pistol and called him. I told him that he needed to come home right away and that I needed him. I waited for him to walk through the door.

The Fourth Wife

Before I could fuck Chris up, my cousin called me and I told him what happened. I told him I was about to fuck Chris up and my cousin begged me to get my things and to start walking, he'll find me. I calmed down and my cousin had a friend of his picked me up until we met.

Chris called me asking if I was okay and where I was? I confronted him and cussed him out about the bullshit I just found out. I told Chris I read everything in his Facebook inbox and he better be glad I left, because he was about to get fucked up! I hung up and he kept calling and texting apologizing. He kept saying, he loved me and would do anything to make it right.

My heart was in crumbles and I did not want to hear any more of his lies. He texted me again, begging to answer the phone. Chris promised to tell me everything, no matter what happens and warned I would hate him even more. Deep down, I wanted to know why he was doing these things to me. I went on and answered the phone (I know, I know!).

"Why do you betray me to your friends, like I'm the bitch that won't let you go anywhere or do anything?"

He says, "I don't know."

"You don't know? You don't want people knowing you have a cool ass down to earth girlfriend?"

The Fourth Wife

Big ***sigh***

He told me the reason he did those things; because he thought he was going to lose me, and he thought I was doing the same thing.

What the fuck? He really said this shit to me and I was livid! He was still being selfish and only thinking about himself.

"Why would you keep putting me through this?"

"Go ahead and tell it all, because it seems to come back to me, anyway."

I was thinking, when he's out with his fraternity brothers, he would pick a fight with me like I was doing something and all along, it was him.

Chris then tells me, he thought we had broken up during our recent trip where he was in Aruba and I was in Jamaica. He even said when I did not come home after my trip and went to Atlanta, he had a threesome with two women.

Y'all, I was so outdone! Can y'all believe this shit? I could not!

"You are the DEVIL, man!"

I hung up really pissed! When I got home, I felt stupid for believing Chris could be the love of my life. I tried to get back on my grind to move on from him. Chris kept calling and texting me for weeks, but I ignored him.

I had a huge birthday party at The Vault and all of my friends showed me so much love and support. Chris told me, he was going to stop by and I abruptly stopped him in his tracks! I strongly advise him not to come if he didn't want to get fucked up. We already had planned a birthday trip to the Bahamas and I was going to go by my damn self. He really wanted to go with me and offered me to have the room and he promised he would not bother me.

"No! I'm good."

One day, he called me and asked if I can come to Huntsville, because it was some things he wanted to release off of his chest.

Y'all know I fell for this bullshit, right?

I got there, he tried to hug me and I wasn't feeling it.

"I'm good, don't touch me!"

"I need to get all of my stuff I left."

He told me, "It's in the room."

The Fourth Wife

Chris kept apologizing and he will do whatever I wanted him to do. He said, he would go on Facebook and apologize to me in front of the whole world. I could not do anything but cry and tell him, he 'killed me on the inside'. He tried to hug me again and I pushed him away.

So, he told me, he had one request and if I can listen.

"What do you want?"

He wanted me to come in the living room, because he had something to show me.

"I don't want anything from you!"

He pleaded for me to come and to close my eyes. Of course, I was very hesitant, but I agreed as he led me to the living room. He advised me not to peep as he guided me to the sofa. Chris sat me down and put something in my hand and he asked if I could figure out what it was? It felt like a seashell. Then, he tells me to open my eyes and Chris was on one knee with a ring.

He asked me to Marry Him!

"Are you serious? Why would I say yes to you, after everything you have done to me?"

"No! I can't marry you, because you don't know what love is!"

Chris responded with, "Teach me how to love you."

"How? I can't teach you how to love someone; it has to be inside of you."

"You only think of yourself and no one else and you are only asking me to marry you, because you fucked up, again!"

I got up and left him sitting there and I headed back to Birmingham. I cried all the way home, because I didn't understand Chris. I mean, how can you not know how to really love someone?

It was getting close to my birthday trip and Chris kept trying to reach out to me. One day, he text, pleading to let him learn how to truly love me and to come on the trip. I thought about it and agreed to let him come on the trip. I advised him to keep his distance and to not push himself on me.

Things were going okay. Chris rented out a restaurant for the two of us with a private Chef. He was doing everything he could to please me. We talked about the proposal and I mentioned to him, I wasn't trying to hurt him or his feelings. I expressed to him that it was wrong, because he was doing it for himself and knew he was going to lose me.

The Fourth Wife

No matter what I'll always love you. I know I'm talking to a brick wall and anything I say will get twisted. Whenever you calm down we can make this right.

I'll do whatever it takes to make this right and no I'm not putting nothing above you wine included.

She accepted me as her king. Well a King who doesn't love, cherish, and protect his Queen is something far less than great. I humbly throw myself at her feet and beg her forgiveness. She has been my ride or die, my strength, my everything. She is everything that is good in my life. Never again will I neglect to love, cherish, and celebrate her. Never again will I willingly allow myself to fail her. She is worth more than life to me and she deserves the best that I have to give. She is my everything and deserves everything that I have to give.

ways dogged out. The Anthony Hamilton song "Pray for Me" keeps playing in my head...funny how I really hated that song and now I get it. It's like you

keep waking up in jail cell after you killed an innocent person. I don't know how to shut my mind down. I'm soooo sorry. I know you will never take me

back and I understand why. At this point I just want to be forgiven. I was told that if I pray and submit, the Lord has a way of turning even our mistak

es into blessings. This guilt keeps me from submitting and I honestly feel like the Lord loves me but he won't help me anyway. I gotta rely on myself to

She is my everything and deserves everything that I have to give. She is my best friend and I will always love and protect her. She is God's gift to me a

nd I promise to treat her like the treasure she is in my life. You are Beautiful, Amazing, and Sexy. Sometimes we are Romeo and Juliet. Sometimes we a

re Ike and Tina. Sometimes we are Bonnie and Clyde. I NEED YOU

I LOVE YOU SOOO MUCH

Lord has a way of turning even our mistak

es into blessings. This guilt keeps me from submitting and I honestly feel like the Lord loves me but he won't help me anyway. I gotta rely on myself to

pull myself out. I only pray that the Lord heals you and gives you peace of mind and turns this situation into a blessing for you. I don't deserve any go

od thing. Your forgiveness would be more than I deserve.

Spoke to my friend about what happened. After she went off on me making me feel even worse she replied, " That don't even sound like you   What hap

pened to the old   ?" Honestly I dont know what I was thinking. Perhaps was tired of playing the good guy, perhaps God doesn't care about me so do w

hatever, perhaps single till marriage, perhaps she is probably doing the same thing, perhaps your bout to propose so one last thing, ...All false ideas

and the bottom line is that Im selfish and a loser and it wasn't worth it. Always prided myself on being the good guy and now I'm the same

to get caught up in the trappings of ego and pride while at the same time neglecting and bringing undue pain and heartache to the people we truly love. I recently had such an experience and left the love of my life in a place of despair and heartache. From that experience I learned that the true measure of a man is the value he places on those who mean the most him and bring the most value to his life. My future wife   is that person to me. She is one of the most compassionate and beautiful people I have ever known. She means more to me than anything the world has to offer. I regret that when I had a chance to celebrate and acknowledge her meaning in my life I failed her. I am not a perfect man but i can honestly say that I am a far better man with her than I would be without her. She used to believe in me and betraying her trust is a fate

Love You Always....I will leave you alone.

U are evil... u don't care about no one but urself... U don't give a fuck about me. I have more screen shots but no need to tex u know who all u fucking flirting with. All I need from u is to just get me bk my 3k for condo in Barbados and whet flights we where gonna be on so I can get a credit... U have a serious problem.. U need to stay single for the rest of ur life because u don't know how to be with 1 Person.. but thanks for fucking my life all the way up. I'll mail u ur key.. don t send me shit changing my shit today.

Ok what about my stuff?

Can I get my stuff and we go our separate ways peacefully?

I don't want to break up

I don't want anyone else

You proved your point

Let me prove forever

Delete that shit you made your point your just gonna keep getting pissed

You went fishing and found something now everything is fucked even stuff that isn't

Tex me the flight information and put my 3k n my account
                    ...Don't tex or call me no more

I will make the payments up to 1,500 as promised beginning August. You can still go on that trip and I'll stay in the other house if you like. I'll f

ind the flight info. I'll try to grab my stuff this weekend and try not to bother you again.

I promise you and I can put my hand on the bible. I have NEVER cheated on you and have no plans to. Not sure what you read but I have been faithful. I h

ave spent all of my free time with you. I go straight there when I get off work and am back here with zero disappearing acts. I acknowledge I have flirt

ed before but I promise I have no desire to cheat on you ever.

Sorry for whatever pissed you off.

Kinda fucked up way to go out. But if you think about it when am I Not with you or trying to be with you

On my way

Oook do you need a ride ...you won't let me talk to you

Not gonna do this over text. Whenever you calm down call me.

Can you please answer your phone

If you answered your phone you would know the whole truth. Right

if you answered your phone you would know the whole truth. Right now you don't know.

I didn't want to do this over text and it will make you more angry but here goes the 100% truth: 1) Per Crazy Chick. There was a chick there with her dude who was hitting him in front of everyone and we were like why the fuck is he with her? That's when I responded that the sex gotta be epic if they are crazy. They all concurred and we been joking. We saw the same chick on the beach and said who is gonna find out how crazy she is and that's how that came about it's a joke....you should know that when I said best ever...top 10...so good she was crying....its a spin off from another convo

someone music fest weekend but (not anyone at the Music fest concert). I felt like shit after. I also slept with someone my first day in PR 2 days before my Son arrived. I lied about that. I also slept with that girl during the NYE trip. I can argue the fact that we didn't go together officially in any of those cases, but at the end of the day I lied about it thinking I was protecting you. This probably makes you feel even worse but it's the truth and I know there is no coming back from this so I may as well own up to it. Since Jan when we agreed to start fresh, I have NEVER cheated on you. And since I know your not coming back I have no reason to lie because this text won't change your mind. I'm In fact it will probably ensure that you're never coming back. YOU ARE MY WORLD. Sorry for the pain

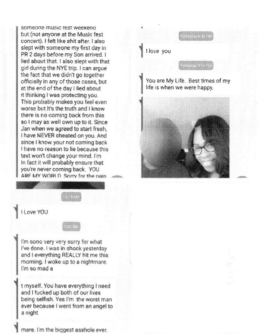

I love you

You are My Life. Best times of my life is when we were happy.

I Love YOU

I'm sooo very very sorry for what I've done. I was in shock yesterday and I everything REALLY hit me this morning. I woke up to a nightmare. I'm so mad a

t myself. You have everything I need and I fucked up both of our lives being selfish. Yes I'm the worst man ever because I went from an angel to a night

mare. I'm the biggest asshole ever.

He still felt some type of way, because I said, no. He was also trying to hold those feelings back, but it did not last long, because the arguments started again. I have never been with a man that loves drama so much, but we made it through the trip even with him trying his best to make it pleasant.

I went into deep meditation and reading the Bible in search of some clarity about Chris, because I was really trying to make this relationship work. I tried forgiving again and it was really rough, but we were working it. We even planned a trip to Barbados with our families.

One day, we went to the mall and visited a jewelry

The Fourth Wife

store. I saw the most beautiful ring ever and told him, if we ever make it, this is it. I wanted it to be the right way.

We get to Barbados, all excited and everyone was having a great time. Chris told me that I was going to be his wife in Barbados, but I didn't really think anything of it. A couple of days passed by and yet again we were back arguing over some bullshit. Chris was putting hearts and fire emojis under women pictures on Instagram.

"What the fuck is wrong with you?"

"How are you with me, saying you love me and why the hell are you still flirting with bitches on social media?"

I didn't speak to him for the rest of the day. Later that night, we were all celebrating his son and sister's birthday. I was in my room still pissed off. Chris comes in and asked me to come into the living room so we can all sing 'Happy Birthday'. I went to the living room with our combined families and we all sang the birthday song. As I sat down, he turned to me and pulls out the ring.

I looked at him like he was crazy as hell! In my mind, I was thinking, "are you fucking kidding me?" I was looking at my daughter in disgust, while he was proposing to me. The fact that he was asking me this in front of his entire family made me even more pissed off! Chris got on his knees saying, he didn't want me to feel pressured, but he was miserable without me and he wanted to marry me. If I said "no", he would have understood, but he wanted me to be his wife.

The weird part about it, his mom must have seen my facial expression of disgust, because she kept telling Chris to wait for my response as he was proposing. I reluctantly said yes, because I didn't want to embarrass him in front of his family. He leaned in and kissed me, but my facial expression still wasn't with it.

While everyone was screaming, "Congratulations" and checking out the ring, my daughter and I were still disgusted about what just happened. I already told her what Chris did earlier that day and we were both like, 'what the fuck?'.

I went back to my room and Chris came in thanking me for agreeing to marry him and promised he would make me happy and stop doing things to hurt me.

"Chris, if you can't change, then this isn't going to work."

He said, "I will and I will start seeing my therapist again, so we can do marriage counseling."

"I think it's the best thing for us to do."

We all left Barbados and it was one of the best places

we ever visited. Back home, I was getting excited about planning our wedding and letting our family and friends know about it. Things were well again for a little awhile. We were invited to Buffalo for an NFL game by one of my celebrity friends. Chris let me go but declined to go in support of Colin Kaepernick and his stance against the NFL.

Before I left, I asked him, "Are you sure I can go and to take my sister with me?" He was fine with it. As soon as he found out I was staying at my celebrity friend house, he lost it and started flipping out on me. He wanted to know why I wasn't at a hotel.

"We always crash at his house! He has enough rooms for everyone."

"My sister and I always crash in a room together."

Chris was still going off on me and I could not understand why. Of course, I'm thinking he's starting this shit again, because he's probably out fucking hoes, again!

I came back home and he acted like nothing happened.

"Please set up an appointment with the therapist for us, because I don't have time for this shit, again!", I asked.

Chris promised he was going to change. Two weeks

later, we went out of town for his birthday and we had a great time. The next couple of months was a roller coaster and I was doing a lot of planning for our wedding. We were busy throughout October, including Magic City Classic and Halloween.

Chris was putting in the work on his winery and making wine. Meanwhile, therapy wasn't helping us, because he would never open up, nor tell the entire truth about anything.

Thanksgiving was at his parent's house and we had a good time enjoying each other with food and movies. By this point, I was constantly traveling back and forth between Birmingham and Huntsville. We were trying to figure out how we can make it work with coming together. I had my club, my house, and family in Birmingham and he had his job in Huntsville. Chris decided to stay in Birmingham and drive to work, since he worked 4 days out of the week.

Christmas was approaching and Chris asked me what I wanted for Christmas.

"I want those Louboutin's Clear Red Bottom shoes."

He told me he wasn't going to pay $600 for a pair of shoes.

"Well, whatever you want to get me."

Christmas was at his parent's house and he decided to

give my gift early. I closed my eyes and he gave me a gift bag. Chris surprised me with a puppy. I had been begging him about getting a Teacup dog, so I asked him if it was a Teacup dog? He said, "no, but it won't get over 3 to 4 pounds."

"As long as he stays under that, I'm good. You spent more on the dog than the shoes!"

"Why couldn't you get what I really wanted?"

Chris adamantly told me, he wasn't spending $600 on those shoes. I was looking at him crazy, because he spent way more on a dog. Okay!

I ended up giving the dog to my Mom, because it wasn't the type of dog I wanted and plus, he ended up weighing about 15 pounds or more! So, Chris got pissed because I gave the dog away and he told me not to ask for shit again!

"Man, I didn't ask for him, you got me what you wanted me to have!"

"I never asked you for shit, not one single thing!"

"When we go on trips, I have to pay for my own flights and half on the hotels or I pay for the fucking hotels!"

Wedding Bliss

January 2018

It's New Years and we went to Dominican Republic and had a great time. On our way back home, we had a layover in Atlanta. While there, I needed a new car, since my car was totaled. I found a great car with a great price, plus it hardly had any miles on it. We drove home with the new car.

My daughter's birthday was coming up and she wanted to go to the cabins with a couple of her girlfriends, her sister and myself. I let Chris know, I was taking them to the cabins. To my surprised, not only did he let me go, but he was going with us!

"Why do you want to go with us?"

"It's only the girls and I that's going on this trip."

Chris didn't want to be home, alone. So, I reluctantly agreed for him to come with us.

All of the girls met at my house, while he drove from Huntsville and we hit the road. We were all excited once we got to the cabin. It was so beautiful, until we saw roaches everywhere!

"Oh, hell no!"

We were moved to another cabin and once we settled in, I didn't see Chris. It was as he disappeared. I found him downstairs, outside on the balcony.

"What are you doing?"

He told me he was taking selfies. So, I went to check on the girls to make sure everyone settled in and we put up the groceries too.

Chris, apparently had disappeared again and I went to look for him. I found him upstairs, outside on the balcony.

"What are you doing, now?"

He said, he was taking selfies.

"Huh? You just told me when we were downstairs, that you were taking selfies."

"It's the same background with dead ass trees and trash out there!"

"Let me see your phone!"

Chris quickly said, "no."

"You told the therapist, anytime I need to see your phone, I could see it. Let me see it!"

He said, no and that he was still taking pictures.

"Here! Take my phone and take as many pictures as you want. You can send them to your phone, once I'm done."

He still said, no!

I snatched Chris phone out of his hands and went into the other bedroom and locked the door. As I sat on the bed browsing through his phone, he broke into the room using a credit card. He jumped on the bed and wrestled with me to get his phone out of my hands. We fell off of the bed onto the floor and when we got up, he had the phone in his hands. I was still trying to get it back from him. Chris pushed me in my chest and ran to the bathroom, locking it behind him.

I blacked out from the push and I managed to kick the door off the hinges. Chris was trying to delete things off of his phone and I started beating his ass! The girls came running in and pulled me off of him. He screamed, "She's crazy" until I told them what happened. The girls asked him, "Why you didn't give her the phone?" Chris replied, "That's my phone, my property and I don't have to give her anything!"

The girls were pissed, because they were already aware of the past cheating and told Chris, "You are engaged to our Mom and you told the therapist, she can see your phone anytime she wanted to, but now she can't?" All he could say, I was crazy and that was his phone. I went into the room where he was and took off the engagement ring.

"The wedding is off!"

Chris locked himself in the room for the rest of the trip.

The girls and I continued to enjoy the trip and I was determined to make the best of it. I didn't want my babies to see how bad I was hurting and how I felt like a damn fool, again! As we were leaving, I went to the back of the van while he drove.

Once we made it back to my house, I threw all of his shit downstairs so he could take it back to Huntsville. I threw the rest of the shit in the trash. I was so hurt and I felt like I was the stupidest woman ever.

The rest of January, I was so depressed and stressed, my body started acting out. It was so bad I had to be rushed to the ER, because I was experiencing different body reactions similar to welts, which was all over my body. My lips and eyes were swelling and I was losing a lot of weight. It's crazy, because I loved that man so much. My body, mind and heart didn't know how to cope without him.

February had passed and when March came around, I couldn't take it anymore. I contacted him and asked, if we could meet halfway. All I wanted was sex, but didn't want him back. At first Chris declined, but changed his mind and we ended up meeting up. I told him, "Don't kiss me, just sex." I started crying while it was happening, because my body was missing him and I thought I could handle it.

Afterwards, he started talking to me about us and I didn't want to go there, because I knew we were going to argue again; in which, we did. We both went our separate ways.

Time has passed and we got back together, again. (I know, I know.) Chris had to travel for his job and he asked me to go on a road trip with him. I agreed to go with him and I was still angry, until he pulled over to a drive-thru animal safari. Instantly, all of my anger went away.

He knew, I loved animals.

Later that night, Chris's phone was blowing up around midnight. He kept trying to send it to voicemail and after it rang the last time, I asked him, "Why are you not answering your phone?" He claimed, he didn't know who it was and that it looked like a spam caller. The phone rang again and I told him to answer it.

Y'all, this fool tried to tell me, it was a telemarketer!

"At this time of night? Stop lying to me!"

"Is it someone you're talking to?"

He said, "yes".

"So, why did you lie about it?"

Chris told me, he wanted this to be perfect and he wanted us to work.

"Does she know this?"

He said, "yes".

"You are lying! You haven't told this woman, we were on this road trip and you probably haven't told her you have been talking to me!"

"Call her back and let her know."

Chris called the woman back and told her that he was with me and he wants to work it out with me. I heard her say, "ok". However, I was still on the fence about him.

Y'all, I know what you're thinking, but I was head over heels for this man! The kicker is, he had already replaced me so quickly!

After coming home from the trip, I told Chris I wasn't sure how this would work, because he was still entertaining other women. I advised him, there would be no reason for us to continue and he won't stop.

Chris replied, "I will do whatever you want me to do

and show you, you're all I need. I want you to be my wife for the rest of my life." I continued to have some faith in him.

The next couple of months were good. I was back to grinding and I was featured in a movie, "Juug Gone Wrong". I received an award for 'Woman of Color and Leadership'. Chris was there supporting me. Even Mother's Day was great! Chris surprised me with a picnic lunch at the Botanical Gardens in Huntsville. I was beginning to fall in love with him again.

It was the annual Aruba trip and I knew what could possible happen there, but I didn't trip, because I was trying to build my trust in him. He went with one of his homies, but in my heart I knew. So, my sister and I decided to go to Haiti on a mission trip, but the trip ended abruptly due to violence that had erupted. We flew to Miami to enjoy the rest of our trip. After Chris's Aruba trip, he ended up crashing my sister and I vacation. I didn't say anything, but we all enjoyed Miami including his son and nephew.

Back home in Birmingham, things were getting hectic. It was time to work with my cousin for his campaign run. Chris and I were doing good spending time with each other, especially since we were both traveling back and forth from Birmingham to Huntsville and vice versa.

One day, I asked Chris if he'd spoken with the woman from our recent road trip. He claimed, she kept calling

The Fourth Wife

him and saying she loves him and thought they were going to be together.

"What the fuck? So, this damn woman says she love you after only you been talking to her for a month and a half?"

"Were you with this woman while we were together?"

He said, "no."

Y'all know I was looking at him, like "nigga please!"

I went on and let it go, because I was getting heated.

I asked Chris was he still talking and texting her, but he stated, "no." (Yeah, right!)

One day, Chris asked if I still wanted to get married? He told me, he loved me and wanted me to be his wife. He also mentioned, "We will have forever for me to show how much I love you." I told Chris, I loved him and let's continue with therapy while we check on the November date we'd originally set.

I called the venue in Birmingham to see if the date was still available. The date was available, since I couldn't get my money back. I told Chris about the date being available. He started talking about one of our first trip, Grenada. This was one of my favorite vacation spots. He then said, "If we could get married there, would you want to do it?"

"Hell yeah! I love that place!"

This man had already checked everything there, including flights, hotel and all. I was really surprised. The date Chris picked was in August, 8-18-2018 to be exact.

"What about my kids and family? I'm not paying that much to fly them out and this is last minute for my family and friends."

Chris said, we didn't need anyone, but us. I thought about it and talked it over with my kids and they were okay with it, so I told him, let's do it. All in all, it was close to $7,000. We paid for our own flights and I made the deposit to Sandals. Chris promised to pay me back, once he got paid.

In July, I had to decide whether I wanted to stay in Birmingham while he drives to Huntsville for work or to move to Huntsville. After we discussed it, I decided to move to Huntsville and help him start a winery there. On the day of my annual birthday bash party, my ass ended up getting food poisoning. I pushed through it, like a 'G', sweating and all.

Once I got better, I contacted a realtor to put my house up for sale and started preparing for my wedding. I went dress shopping with my immediate family and close friend. I didn't tell anyone else; we were going to get married. I ended up paying for the full trip and Chris promised to pay his half once we got back from Grenada.

I paid for the damn wedding.

When we got to Grenada, I felt like a princess and everything was beautiful. As Chris was saying his vows to me, I saw a tear fall. That did it for me, because this man has never cried around me or never showed this side of him. My heart was full and I was in love with this man. I just knew I was going to spend the rest of my life with him. Whenever Chris smiled, my heart would smile. The photographer had our photos ready the next day, after I paid him to expedite it.

We received our disc and watched our wedding photos in the room and I couldn't do anything, but cry. I loved every bit of it. I didn't want to leave Grenada; I could have stayed there, forever. We made it back home and I prepared to transition to Huntsville.

The butterflies did not last long, at all! I was hit with a rude awakening, because Chris turned into someone I did not know, or he was really showing the real side of him! It was like living with Dr. Jekyll and Mr. Hyde! He was adamant on me changing my name on my driver's license and I told him, I was going to handle it. This happened within the same week from our wedding.

We woke up one morning and he said to c'mon, let's go. I'm thinking we were going somewhere to eat.

Chris took my ass to the Social Security Administration to change my name, then took me to the DMV to change my name on my driver's license. On top of that, he was pissed off, because I kept my last name and added his. During his tantrum, he said, "Why are you still trying to live your old life? You are my wife now and you need to leave Birmingham and your old life behind!"

"I still have a life and business there! That's why I kept my last name on there!"

I believe Chris acted like he didn't get it but wanted to have his way. We walked across the hall so we could get our marriage license on file for the State of Alabama. I was mad as hell, because I told him, I was going to handle it. The fact that he drove all over Huntsville after coming back from our wedding trip didn't make sense to me. Hell, everyone knew we got married. We already posted on social media on our flight from Grenada.

I got my youngest daughter an apartment in Birmingham, since I was moving to Huntsville, including my furniture. Chris gave his old furniture to her, while I got her a new bed and kitchen set. We moved all of my belongings to Huntsville and put the rest in storage, because Chris apartment was too small. My bathroom at my house was bigger than his whole apartment, but I wasn't tripping. I told him I was good for a couple of months, then we can focus on finding a house.

The Fourth Wife

In September, we went to the Virgin Islands and it was beautiful and we had a great time. When we got home, we started planning for his birthday party/wine fest. I wanted to make sure Chris had a great birthday party. I bought all the food and cake, because he spent all of his money on getting the wine ready.

I was on my best behavior, because I didn't know a lot of people there, especially, the women. My sister and brother-in-law came in to support and she complimented me for staying calm, because some of these chicks would have gotten snatched up!

"I'm trying to be a better me."

I don't do new friends and especially with his past, I didn't trust this shit, anyway. This one chick in particular, I tried to speak to her and her ass didn't speak back. She was all over Chris, taking pictures everywhere. After we left the party, we all went to Club Envy and there she was again. I asked him, "Who is this chick?"

"I remember, she came to Birmingham when I did your wine fest at The Vault and now, she's here again at your birthday party!"

"She is rolling her eyes and not speaking!"

Chris acted like he didn't know her and didn't know why she was acting that way to me.

"I will drag her ass all up through this club, because I don't have time for mess and stupid bitches you have been with or fucked!"

We abruptly left, because he knew I wasn't playing. I remembered, Chris told me, he didn't fuck with the locals, because all of the women he knows in Huntsville are messy, miserable and fucking each other men. I knew I didn't want to hang out with anyone there and especially with the fake ass women he may have been involved with.

In October, it was time for my alumni week and it seems like whenever I go back to Birmingham, Chris would get an attitude for no reason. One day before I left, I was in the bathroom while he came home and went outside on the deck to smoke a cigar. He didn't know I sat on the sofa and I overheard him telling someone, he had to add me and my kids to his insurance. I was so furious, because my oldest daughter had her own insurance and my youngest daughter was added to mine.

The crazy part is, he's the one suggested to add us on his insurance as a backup to mine. This nigga was telling people basically, I was begging to be added to his. When his ass came in, I asked him, "Why are you lying like that?" He was shocked and looking stupid as hell.

"I have never asked you to do anything for me or my kids and that's the reason why, because of lying shit like that!"

"I will never give you a reason to say, you did shit for me, because this has happened to me in the past!"

"I'll be damned if I ever let it come out of anybody else lips, but you're supposed to be my husband and you're out here talking about me and my kids, like we're a fucking charity case!"

"Fool, I been doing this by myself for years without anybody, so don't you ever put my name in your mouth!"

He was doing all of this for gossip and on top of that, he always loved to start mess. Literally, he'd gossip about everyone and loved drama like a fucking woman. It was as he lived for it. Chris talked about everyone from his fraternity brothers, friends, ex-girlfriends, and family.

He would be on the phone with one sister talking about the other one, then call the other sister to talk about her. Chris got mad at me, because I didn't want to hear it, nor be a part of it. I swear, I felt like the dude in the marriage and he was the chick. There was one chick he would always crack on that was supposed to be his friend, but I felt, he was fucking her.

Chris kept insulting about people who would get gastric bypass to lose weight, only to turn around and gain it back. He thought it was hilarious by them wasting their time and money on the process. Even with all of that, my issue was him and these hoes he claimed I accused him of being with.

Alumni week was great and I enjoyed catching up with old friends. The rest of October were busy with events at Chattanooga Cigar Lounge and Magic City Classic promoting the winery. My first granddaughter was born by the end of the month and it was a great month.

There were some roller coaster moments in November and of course my late celebrity friend's birthday. We also celebrated my grandson birthday and took all of the kids and grandkids to Orlando, Florida. It was a great family vacation. The grandkids loved their "Pop Pop" and he always did something with them. He's been around all of them since they were born.

My celebrity blues singer brother had a concert in December and we caught up with him. We had a blast at the concert. Chris and I were doing okay for about two weeks, but then here comes the drama again with him. I really felt like he loved to pick fights with me. He simply didn't know how to live a happy life, because it was filled with drama and mess.

For our annual Christmas shindig, his whole family and my daughter went to Gaylord Opryland Hotel in Nashville, Tennessee. We had a great time with family

The Fourth Wife

photoshoot, hitting up every bar and we took advantage of everything the hotel offered. We did our own special, "25 bars of Christmas". There was supposed to be 1 drink or 1 shot limit, but we took up to 4 at some spots and I passed out, face down! Merry Christmas, LOL!

The Saga

Chris and I brought in the New Year 2019 in Cancun. After coming home, life was back to normal with the same petty arguments. We were still going to therapy, but it didn't seem to help. January has always been a hard month for Chris every year. I tried my best to comfort him and he seemed to get better over the years. My youngest daughter wanted to go back to Gaylord Opryland for her birthday and we did. It wasn't long before the drama started again. Chris and I argued so badly, you could hear us all the way down the hallway at the hotel.

Y'all, I didn't understand why this was happening all of the time. I just wish we could at least go for a month or hell the rest of our lives without the stupid shit. I refused to let this mess up another one of my baby's birthday. Majority of the time, it was about him and social media shit.

Once we got back home, we started working on getting a building for the winery and also to find a house. I could not stay in that damn apartment any longer! Hell, when the gofer rats bigger than cats start breaking in shit, it's time to go and let them have the

The Fourth Wife

whole apartment!

Chris and I planned to go to Costa Rica for Valentine's Day. On the day of the trip, he usually wakes up early to go to work, while I'm still knocked out in bed. I was awakened by a phone call from a wrong number and it was hard to go back to sleep, I called Chris's cell. I didn't get any answer, so I called his office number and it went to voicemail. After calling and texting, I still didn't get any response.

At this point, I was really concerned and scared something happened. He always has his phone on him, even when he's in a meeting at work. He normally would send quick texts if he couldn't answer his phone. I freaked out, because I lost someone close to me before and was devastated for a long time. I wanted to hear from him to make sure he was okay. I called his immediate family and they couldn't reach him either.

After about an hour, he finally called and told me he was at the barbershop getting a haircut and he put his phone in his luggage for the trip.

BRUH! I was so furious, because he always has his phone with him. Since he was on call from work, he would sneak away from work sometimes. I knew it was all bullshit and I was so pissed and I canceled the trip.

"You can go on the trip by yourself!"

I hung up! Chris rushed home asking me, was I ready?

"Hell no, I'm not ready! I told you, I'm not going!"

Next thing I know, he called me a "Bitch" and said, "fuck you!"

"Ain't no fucking way you were without your cell phone for over an hour! Knowing you left your job too; do I really look that damn stupid?"

He said, "Ain't no other women checking for him".

"I know you're lying now!"

Chris blew the fuck up and screamed, "You! Stupid bitch! You want to see cheating; I'm going to show your ass cheating!"

He left and didn't come back home, until the next day. Meanwhile, I drove back to Birmingham the next morning and chilled for a few hours to calm down. I decided to drive back to Huntsville and on my way, I received a text from him apologizing about everything he said. He promised he wasn't with anyone and stayed at a hotel by himself on Valentine night.

Chris was so angry and upset, because he lost money by not going to Costa Rica. He asked me to come home and promised to make it all right and to redo Valentine's Day. Chris didn't know I was already en route to the apartment. When I got there, he was

The Fourth Wife

sitting on the sofa, apologizing for everything again. He gave me a card and wished me a, "Happy Valentine's Day". I didn't open the card, because I was so numb, hurt, and angry.

This was the day I fell out of love with my husband.

We barely had any words for each other for a long time. I continued seeing my therapist and she mentioned I needed to focus on myself and happiness, because I didn't deserve this. It's weird thinking how he used to go to therapy with me and whenever my therapist would ask him questions, he'd immediately deflect.

In one session, I told her an issue I had with him doing and instead of him fully listening to what I was saying, he pointed out, I smoke weed.

"OMG! What the fuck, man?"

"What does that have to do with what I'm saying?"

Again, Chris constantly deflected the situation off of him. I told him, I tell my therapist everything about me, including the weed.

"Hell, the main reason why I smoked, because you're stressing me the hell out!"

Of course, he was looking stupid as hell.

In another session, not long after we got married, he didn't want me to wear my open-heart necklace anymore. Chris was upset, because an ex gave it to me.

"Are you serious? We have been together for years and you never had any problem, until now!"

I mentioned to Chris in the past, majority of my wardrobe, shoes and purses are gifts. So, now you choose to argue over my necklace! I never had any issues with shit he received in the past.

A week later, Chris's dad called and asked to take me out for lunch. We went and talked about a lot of things, especially Chris and I relationship. He promised, his son wasn't with another woman on Valentine's Day.

"I still don't believe it."

The following week, I decided to go on to Costa Rica, since we still had our flights and I was able to get another hotel. On our way to Costa Rica, we had a layover in Florida and once we got to our destination, I opted for double beds. I didn't want to sleep with Chris, because deep down I know he was with another woman on Valentine's Day.

I was laying in my bed trying to go to sleep, because I was tired. He got in my bed and saying he wanted to hold me. While he was holding me, he apologized again and professing his love for me. Chris acknowledged, he should have never left the apartment and pleaded me to forgive him.

At this point, I started crying as he was caressing and kissing me. He asked to make love to me, because he missed being with me.

My horny ass let him do it. (Shit, I needed love too.)

Costa Rica was a decent trip and even though I enjoyed the country and its amenities, but the connection to Chris was lost. I wasn't feeling him. He was trying to be nice, but it felt forced. After we left, we spent two additional days in Orlando, Florida visiting different animal places.

Back home in Huntsville, things were the same. The arguments got worse. On top of the ongoing issues, Chris didn't want to take my advice whenever it came to the winery.

"I have had my own club for more than seven years and this is what I know and do!"

He still did whatever he wanted to do concerning the winery.

On a brighter note, we put a bid on a house that I found and we got it with a pool as well. This was the best news for me in a long time, because I was ready to put those damn gofer rats behind me! (Thank you, Lord!) So, on closing day, we were getting ready and I put on some tights with a long sleeve V-neck shirt and boots. While putting on makeup and fixing my hair, I saw him in the mirror looking "shob". I complimented how good he looked and he didn't respond to any of it. Instead, he went off on me and asked if I was really wearing my outfit?

"What do you mean?"

"Didn't you wear those tights, yesterday?", he asked.

"Yes, only for a minute to run a quick errand and I took them off when I came home."

All of a sudden, Chris berated me on how I was embarrassing him and he couldn't take me anywhere with him. I was furious and confused at the same time.

"What the fuck are you talking about?"

He kept attacking me and I was clueless. The only thing I thought of was, by him wearing a shiny ass silk suit, he expected me to wear a ball gown or something. We ended up driving separate cars to the closing and once we finished signing the papers, I went to the apartment by myself. I didn't want to go to the house with him at all. This was supposed to be a celebration, but to me it wasn't.

Our marriage was full of shit and fake to me at this point. The arguments got so bad, he started saying

The Fourth Wife

crazy shit to me and acted like he didn't remember. I suggested, we should see a neurologist to check both of our heads. Chris agreed and we both passed the tests. He got pissed, because he felt, he paid the copay in vain.

"It wasn't for nothing. I'm trying to see what's wrong to help save our marriage!"

Chris wasn't even trying anymore, he even stopped seeing his therapist.

We started talking about the house and the mortgage. Chris couldn't pay the mortgage on his own and needed me to pay half of it plus utilities. His plan was to have it all paid for with the winery once it opened. The problem was I haven't worked in over a year and I had a car note with insurance that he didn't help me with. Chris only had his car insurance and I used my savings to pay for everything. I felt like I had a fucking roommate with benefits!

One day after my therapy session, she provided a list of some things I wanted Chris to improve on. Y'all, he didn't want to do it. He said, "I don't think I can do any of it." Some of the suggestions were: to tell me, you love me, every once in a while, and to see another therapist for himself and etc.

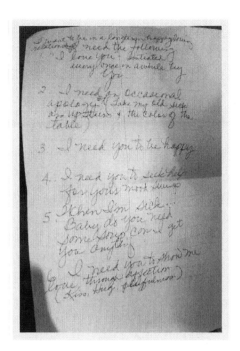

We went down the street for drinks later to discuss
the list. After he expressed his thoughts on the list, I
asked, "Why am I here? Why did I sell my house,
leave my kids and my business to be with you? This is
what I get?"

"Why am I here?"

"Why do you want me here?"

Chris looked at me and couldn't even answer. That
shit hurt so bad and all I could mustered up to say,
"I'm ready to go back to the house."

The next day, he came home from work with roses and a card trying to express how he felt about me. It was getting to the point where, he no longer apologized for doing dumb shit or he stopped saying he loved me. The affection wasn't there anymore. I felt lost and trapped in this marriage.

Around Mother's Day, Chris was trying to be nice and suggested inviting my sisters and mom over for BBQ. It was great seeing everyone including my kids and grandkids. I interacted with my family, since he and I wasn't on good terms.

The following week, Chris's son graduated from high school and we were all proud of him. For his graduation present, we took him, Chris's nephew and my daughter to Miami for a couple of days, then flew out to Cartagena Colombia. Everything was so beautiful there.

I received a text from my nephew, asking if he can stay with us in Huntsville until his apartment was ready. He recently graduated from college and landed a great job. I spoked with my husband about it and we agreed to let him stay. We were all having a great time, until one night, we were discussing airplane mode on the cell phone. Chris's son said, "If your phone is on airplane mode, you can't receive texts or calls." Then Chris replied, "Yes, you can."

Everyone looked at him crazy and we all told him, "No, you can't!" He proceeded by saying, he has his phone on airplane mode all of the time.

"Why do you have your phone on airplane mode at home?"

He was so pissed and told me I was reaching and insecure.

"I'm never insecure about shit!"

"Google, can you receive calls or texts on your phone with airplane mode?"

Of course, Google said, no! Chris was so furious and we started arguing in front of the kids. He left out and I apologized to the kids and we were good. My daughter requested salmon and rice, so I cooked it for her and the boys. I slept on the sofa for the night.

The next day, I didn't want to be bothered with Chris, so him and the kids went sightseeing in Cartagena. I hated I miss seeing more of the country, but hell, I can always go back. After a couple more days in Colombia, we flew back to Orlando, Florida and stayed in a beach resort for a couple more days. We were barely communicating with one another and no one was talking to him for real.

Chris tried letting go of his shitty attitude and decided to cook for us, right when I was getting ready to order some food. We were all sitting at the table eating and joking around and he started tripping again, because no one thanked him for cooking.

"Are you serious, Chris? I told you, I could have ordered something!"

"Why are you mad? Cause' no one said thanks for cooking?"

"You did that on your own and I would never tell people to thank me for cooking."

We all said it was good. As I told the kids to go swimming, he got madder and made his point by saying, I cooked for my daughter in Cartagena and I barely cook for him when we're home.

"I told you years ago, I don't cook anymore, but I will cook every once in a while."

Chris knew this before we got married and I told him, I'll cook more. The fact that he was jealous of me cooking for my child had me so furious! It was so bad; I left and went to the pool and called one of my friends, who is a therapist. I was heated and wanted to beat the shit out of him, because I was at my wits' end with him from the whole damn vacation.

My friend was able to calm me down. I can't do this shit anymore and I was getting a divorce, because Chris is driving me crazy. There is no way, he can love me and treat and talk to me the way he does. Then my friend said, "Divorce is not an option, you love him and I know he loves you."

"SHIIIIIIIDDD!"

"I can't tell!"

My friend suggested to try to enjoy the rest of the trip, and I'll counsel you both when you both come back. I agreed and went in the pool with the kids. We headed back on the road and tried to take the kids to the zoo, but it was packed. We ended up taking them to Gatorland. The rest of the trip was good and we made it home.

The following weekend, one of my celebrity comedian friends was in town for a show. I told Chris, we were going to the show to support him. As I was getting ready, he told me, he wasn't going and the attitude was

The Fourth Wife

back. I finished getting ready and left for the show. I had so much fun and my comedian friends had me laughing all night! I even helped one of my comedian friends sell his T-Shirts after the show. I'm always supporting by creating videos, posting pictures or promoting them. It was a good night.

The next day, Chris was at it again with his bullshit! "Why the hell did you have your breasts out in that dress?", he screamed! Chris went on to say, "He was all up on you in the video and you had your arms around him!"

"First of all, you saw what the fuck I had on last night and if my husband came with me, it wouldn't have been no problem!"

"Secondly, my arm wasn't around him, I was moving him back, because he was about to trip over the suitcase with the T-Shirts!"

"My friend shouted out the winery, so why don't you go back and look at the video again, because you're lying your ass off right now!"

Chris didn't have nothing else to say!

We went to my friend, the therapist for a session and Chris still didn't get it. The whole week was horrible. He kept asking, when was my nephew apartment going to be ready? He was acting like my nephew didn't have a job and was just crashing the house.

"He can stay as long as he need to! This boy goes to work every day and don't eat shit out of our fridge and you barely see him!"

"What's the problem?"

Chris assumed a chick he knew got my nephew the job and thought my nephew wasn't appreciative.

"That's bullshit! My kids and my nephews were not raised like that. They will always thank you for anything you do for them."

Later, I found out my nephew's dad friend connected him with the job and when I told Chris, he was looking crazy, as usual. I'm thinking he'd probably fucked the chick, since he was so concerned about the situation. He knows women from all over. I found out how he got his connects, but I'll save it for later.

One day, I had to pick up the winery sofas from The Vault in Birmingham and I got his son and my daughter's boyfriend to come help me put them in storage in Huntsville. It was hot as hell outside and when we finished, my daughter and her boyfriend went swimming in the pool.

Chris came home to the patio, while I was tending to my roses and I noticed he was saying something to my daughter's boyfriend and they went inside the house. Chris asked him what was his plan for my daughter? The boyfriend responded, "I don't have any right now." Chris rudely told him, "I can't respect you. I wished you never met her, then."

If Chris talked to the boyfriend the right way, he would have found out that he takes care of his family (mom, son, and little brother). Instead, the boyfriend left the house abruptly and my daughter caught up with him. Chris came outside next to me and I asked what was going on?

He told me, he expressed how he felt and was trying to help the boyfriend.

"You don't' know how to talk to people!"

Then he tells me, "This is my house!"

"Just because it's your house, it doesn't give you the right to talk to people any kind of way!"

I called my daughter to come back and promised Chris wasn't going to say anything else to them and I meant that shit! I told Chris, "How are you going to call yourself helping him and attacking the boy at the same time?" As usual, he was looking stupid as fuck!

I drove to Birmingham for a doctor's appointment and while there, Chris called me, asking if I knew my daughter was at the house? I said, "Yes, why?" Chris demanded, he needed to know when someone is in his house! My doctor and I was looking crazy as hell and I told him, I will call him back once the appointment was over. As soon as I got to the car, I called his ass and went the fuck off!

"I don't have to tell you shit! That's my daughter and if I told her to go there and get something or do something for me, then I don't need to call you!"

"This my house as well and this is my daughter and your step-daughter! What the fuck is wrong with you?"

He was so mad and yelled, "It's called a fucking courtesy!" I hung up, because I was so over it!

We took his son back home to Nashville, Tennessee and afterwards, we went to the zoo. We also did some sightseeing and had a good time. Back home, we were finally able to have our counseling session with my therapist friend. I thought we were making some progress, but not to Chris. He stated, I was accusing him and that I called him a monster! He wanted to know why would I call him that?

I explained to Chris, I was stating the truth and if he sees himself as a monster, then it was on him. All I wanted, was for him to be a better man.

Near the end of June, my nephew was able to move into his new apartment and the house was quiet. One day, we were at the pool and talking. I brought up one of my rap artist friend's name and that I was thinking about flying up to New York to ask him if he would work with my nephew, who I manage. Chris abruptly got up and put his clothes on and left without saying anything.

My birthday was approaching and we were trying to figure out where to go. He surprised me to an all paid trip to Aruba and I didn't have to pay for anything, including hotel and flight. We went all over Aruba, since he knew it well from previous visits. It was a great birthday trip. On our way back home, he wasn't feeling good and my daughter was sick as well. I rushed her to the hospital due to asthma.

Nothing was changing in our marriage and it was getting worse by the week. I caught the flu in the midst of it all. I received a text from Chris telling me he was going out for drinks with the guys. Later, he texts me asking if I was clean and I was confused at first, but he wanted some ass.

I was still weak from the flu and could barely move, so I took a shower and put on some lingerie. He came home, sloppy drunk! I have never seen him this drunk before and he was talking loudly.

"Can you not talk so loud? You're hurting my head!"

He yelled, "Well, why don't you go find a man with the right voice, then!"

"What are you talking about? I didn't do all of this for you to be talking crazy to me!"

I watched TV while he was lying next to me on his phone. When Chris passed out, I proceeded to cover him up and he tells me, "Don't touch me and only my woman can touch me!"

"What the fuck did you just say to me?"

He said, "You heard me!"

I pushed is his ass off of the bed and he fell on the floor!

"What the fuck did you say to me? Your wife?"

He didn't reply, so I went to the closet and grabbed our sex paddle and popped his ass. He didn't move, so I popped him again and he replied, "Stop hitting me!"

"What fucking woman?"

The Fourth Wife

He still didn't respond and I hit his ass, again!

Y'all, he has hit my ass way harder, using the paddle during our freaky nights…

All of a sudden, Chris jumped up and pushed my back into the rack in the closet! He was still holding my arms and I tried to push him off of me, then he snatched the paddle and punched me in my face, like I was a man! I was in shock, because he has never hit me before. He took off and locked himself in one of the other bedrooms. I was so furious at this point, because he burst my lip and loosened my tooth.

I got my gun, because I was about to fuck him up, but I thought about my therapist friend who was counseling us. I called him and he was able to calm me down. I couldn't sleep, because I was still sick with the flu and my body was hurting, plus my face was hurting. This was the night I took my married name off of Facebook and went back to my maiden name.

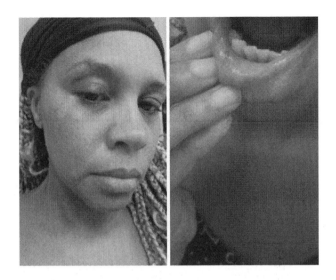

Chris woke up the next morning, telling someone over the phone I jumped him and beat him with the paddle from the night before. His sister and her husband came over for the weekend and I stayed in the room. Chris came into the room sitting at the foot of the bed. He asked, if I was ready to talk?

"I don't have shit to say to you!"

He said, "Why did you hit me?"

"Motherfucker, why don't you go ask your other woman, like you told me last night! Then, you punched me in my fucking face!"

He looked up at me and denied he did this to me. I showed him my bruises on my face, lip and my loose tooth. Chris apologized and claimed he didn't remember any of it.

69   *The Fourth Wife*

"But! You can remember enough to tell people, I jumped on you last night, though!"

"Leave me alone!"

He left and came back with roses.

"I don't want no damn flowers!"

Chris was pissed and yelled, "That's why your ex-husband used to beat your ass, because you made him do it!"

At this point, I went to the patio in an attempt to clear my mind, but he followed me. I went back upstairs and he followed me to apologize for bringing up my past. "It didn't have anything to do with us.", said Chris.

The following week, Chris threw his son a birthday pool party at the house. We were not talking to each other and simply was not on good terms. Both of my daughters and 3 grandkids came along with Chris's whole family. Everyone seemed to get along and it was a nice day.

Chris's dad and I were talking and I told him everything about that night. He told me, "You're not the same person I met and you're not the happy vibrant person you used to be. Don't let anyone change who you are, even if it's my son. Do what will make you happy and back to being you." My older daughter told his dad, "If Chris ever put his hands on my Mom again, he won't be around anymore!"

I went through a domestic violence marriage with my children's dad. We were together for 10 years, then married for 5 years. I went through this bullshit for 15 years and I promised myself, I would never allow another man to put his hands on me. It was nothing, but God's grace that saved Chris's life that night.

His dad tried to build my spirit up by dancing with him and by smiling.

One day, Chris text me, he saw on social media, I wanted a divorce. He got mad, because he finally saw where I removed his last name off of my profile on Facebook.

"That was the night you hit me and I couldn't change it back until 60 days."

I screenshot it and sent it to him. It didn't matter to Chris, he was still pissed. He said he was ready for a divorce, because he didn't want the public to see anything wrong with our marriage. In reality, it was fucked up. When Chris came home, he accused me of having him followed and he thought I was using a spy camera. He was definitely paranoid.

"You are not worth spending money spying on your ass!"

The Fourth Wife

"Fool, you tell on yourself, EVERY TIME!"

The mini cam he was referring to, I ordered it back in 2017 for The Vault. I found out one of my employees was stealing money from me. I text Chris the screenshot from Amazon to him. This fool then says, I was going to get him killed!

"You are not worth me losing my family, nor my life for your dumb selfish ass!"

Chris was a pain in my ass for his bullshit. My body was hurting badly, dealing with arthritis in both of my knees and back. The stress even had my fibromyalgia on fire! I tried to minimize my stress level, but the constant arguments didn't make it any better.

He came home one day from work and he was so angry and moody.

"What's wrong now?"

Chris went in on my ass and calling me all kind of names, then he said, "If you want to go, then leave!"

"What is wrong with you? Where is all of this coming from?"

He finally told me, his shit was backed up and it was hurting.

"You could have said this, instead of going off!"

As a wife, I tried my best to be there for him, even though he was putting me through hell. So, I told him to come on and we went upstairs as he released himself in me. Afterwards, I got dressed and went to my therapy appointment.

I cried the whole way there and when I went into the room, my therapist asked what was wrong. I told her what happened and she let me know, it was a form of rape.

"No, I told him to come on."

"But! Were you engaging to it?", she asked.

"No, I was tired of his attitude towards me."

My therapist broke down why and how it was a form of rape. When I got home, Chris's attitude was gone, like it never happened. He asked me where I wanted to go for our first-year anniversary. I didn't know, because we just came back from Aruba and we didn't need to spend any more money.

I saw my celebrity friend (big bro) was going to be in Nashville for a concert, so I suggested we go there and stay at our favorite hotel while go to the concert. He agreed. The petty arguments were getting worse and he refused to stop until I reacted and got angry. I was trying to stay cool, since it was getting close to our anniversary trip.

On our way to Nashville, we stopped by a winery and a small botanical garden. When we made it to Gaylord Opryland Hotel, Chris was tired and went to sleep. Around 10:30pm, I woke him up so we could go eat. We missed having a romantic dinner due to the restaurants being closed, so I ate a damn cheeseburger.

We got back to our room and celebrated with cake and wine. I went to take a shower and put on something very sexy for him, meanwhile he went and took a shower as well. Chris came out and I laid on his chest in the bed and I closed my eyes for about 20 minutes. I got up and started kissing all over him and got on top of him. He abruptly interrupted me and told me he was good and to lay down and rest.

"Shit! I'm good, it's our anniversary!"

I started kissing on him again and then Chris had the audacity to tell me he took care of himself already.

"Huh? Are you fucking serious?"

I turned over madder than a motherfucker!

The next day, we went to another hotel closer to the arena for the concert. I was getting ready and all of a sudden, Chris decided he wasn't going to the concert.

"Are you serious? This is one of the reasons why we're here! It's for our anniversary."

I went on to the concert and enjoyed myself, but when I came back to the hotel, Chris went to the Cheesecake Factory and swimming at the hotel.

Bullshit! Straight bullshit.

Chris and I made it home and that night, I posted all of my pictures and videos from the concert. The following day, I received a text from him, accusing me of sitting in my celebrity friend's lap. As I attempted to defend myself, he kept interrupting me and not hearing anything I was saying. Chris kept going off on me, by saying I was thirsty for attention based off of my Facebook profile picture.

"Are you serious?"

"Dude! This picture has been up for weeks and you never said anything about it!"

"In fact, I posted the same picture in April and you liked it!"

"So, what the hell is going on?"

Chris was still going off on me saying I'm married and I was disrespecting him with the pictures I posted. He changed his profile picture to indicate he was single and not married. I showed him my profile still shows I was married to him and he was furious, because he was in the wrong.

Ain't nobody disrespected ur ass. If u didn't like the DJ pic I took it down. No one else saw a problem with it cause I asked. Wasn't shit disrespectful about jj, I moved his drunk ass bk to keep from Tripping over the suitcase. I wasn't sitting in   lap. U changed all ur shit and blocked me .no victim here I never claimed that shit at all.

ok cool let's agree to disagree. I'm tired of trying to get you to understand basic etiquette. I can't deal with the disrespect...and tired of arguing about the same shit. If you don't understand the difference between being respectful and being extra over and over I cant be more clear. you still bringing up blocking you when you know damn well it's an issue you started by putting everyone in our personal business. Stop playing victim.

What the FUCK did I put out about us on social media. Not shit. Ur ass blocked me and changed ur shit so please dont go there. Kiss my ass cause u are wrong AF.
Read 2:38 PM

I knew this was coming. 3:15 PM

You're perfect I'm the problem it's cool. 3:16 PM

zero accountability 2:38 PM

No ur ass crazy, bipolar and lying. I'm still waiting on that shit that I know I didn't say
Read 3:16 PM

And deleted my pic so go to hell and don't say shit else to me.
Read 2:39 PM

I'm not about to inbox anyone to follow up on your shit. If I wanted to entertain our mess with random people I would have responded. I dont operate like that. 3:19 PM

U ain't doing shit right as a husband... MF I gave my whole life up for u
Read 2:40 PM

You posted something about dont be telling my husband....I didn't see it but they inboxed me about it and I'm sick of it. I blocked that nonsense...I have to find out via FB that my wife no longer wants to be take accountability 2:41 PM

My problems with you is no their business. I bring it to you. 3:20 PM

Well ur ass should have looked cause I never said shit about us. The only thing I did was took   off and I explained to u y. I didn't say shit about u or us
Read 3:20 PM

Mf when u punched me n the face I deleted   I never posted anything about our marriage or u on fb. Please show me what I said have them to resend it to u cause that is a MF lie. I didn't post shit like that.
Read 2:42 PM

U didn't bring shit to me until now and like I said I didn't say shit about us. I posted my bday pics and just changed my profile pic a week ago. All my shit u n all was up on my sh
Read 3:21 PM

"I want a divorce!"

I couldn't take it anymore and I started on the paperwork to get an uncontested divorce. While I was filling out the paperwork, I was looking for our marriage license. I found it in Chris's paperwork with all of the other divorces and to my surprise, the 3rd wife he married for a split second, was actually his 2nd wife. The 2nd wife he stated, was actually his 3rd wife. I was fucked up about it, because Chris has been lying to me from the beginning. I started packing all of my shit and put it all in the dining room.

It was crazy being in the house. Chris turned the alarm and cable off, then the following week, he turned the WIFI off and I watched Netflix using my data on my phone. I was beyond miserable and within this time, I slept with him one last time. A week later, Chris wanted me to have sex with him, again. I told him, no.

He implied; I wasn't satisfying him in our marriage.

The Fourth Wife

That was bullshit!

"I stop going down on you, because I got tired of smelling shit in my face!"

"Why didn't you tell me?", Chris asked.

"Why the fuck should I have to tell a grown ass man to wash his ass?"

So, no I wasn't going down on him anymore for shit surprises, unless I knew he was clean. Furthermore, I stopped doing all of my freaky shit with my toys, because I didn't feel the way I used to about him, nor bring that side of me out. As a matter fact, I introduced him to 'The 50 Shades of Grey' shit.

August 30, the day we went to file for the divorce and I parked behind him, down from the courthouse. After filing and walking toward to sign the papers, Chris kept saying, he didn't want to get a divorce. He stated, whatever gives me peace, he'll sign it.

As we headed to our cars, I got in mine and the tire light was on. I got out and my damn tire had a flat. I honked my horn at him and as he opened the door, I told him my tire is flat. He literally looked at me, smiled, closed his door and drove off leaving me stranded. I got back in my car and cried. At that moment, God was showing me, I did the right thing filing a divorce from him. I wiped my tears and thanked God and called for help.

A man tried to help me, but his lug wrench didn't fit my tires, so I called a tow truck. About 40 minutes later, Chris text me asking if I changed the tire and he was on his way. Then he was sorry for leaving me there, but he was tired of doing something for someone who didn't want to be with him, anymore. Y'all, I did not respond to that bullshit text! The tow truck came and the man looked at the tire and said, he could fix it.

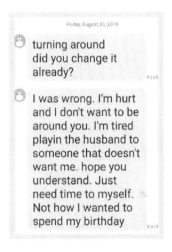

It was a hole in my damn tire, as if someone stabbed it. The man plugged it and I went back to the house and started loading my things up. Chris went through my luggage and took all of my sex toys and I didn't know until I left.

The next day, my daughter, her boyfriend, my nephew, and his girlfriend helped me move the hell out of Huntsville. I stayed at my close friend's house, until my apartment was ready. I was so glad to be back home in Birmingham, but I was so broken on the inside.

By September, Chris and I were not communicating at all, but he turned everything back on and kicked me off the streaming services accounts (Netflix, Spotify, and etc). He forgot to removed me from the cameras at the house. A couple of days later, I'm getting alerts from the house. I saw the most horrendous, gut wrenching thing ever! I had to watch my husband with women going in and out of our house and some days, two women.

The stuff I saw every day, was just ugh. My husband was doing what he does best and wasn't even using protection. I watched this shit live, but I made sure to screenshot all of it, in case of any problem comes up with the divorce. He already had me replaced way before I left Huntsville.

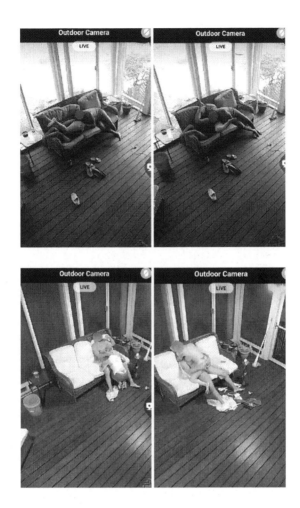

I saw he was on the phone with his cousin bragging about his 2020 boo. All I could do was to shake my head at this bullshit. It's a damn shame, because Chris will never be faithful to anyone. He isn't loyal to his family and friends, literally no one! He only uses people to see what he can get out of them.

The Fourth Wife

Those same hoes I mentioned to him about were the same ones at my house. There was so much shit I went through dealing with him.

The Rundown

August 2019

The night he hit me; he was messaging two bitches…

I figured out his game, he would flirt with them, then fuck them. Chris would keep them in his back pocket whenever he needed them…

Remember when he went M.I.A. on Valentine's Day? That motherfucker was out cheating on me. (I know, I know.)

Recently, my grandkids asked about their Pop Pop and it hurt my heart to tell them he won't be around anymore and he is gone. I told them I will always be there for them. I hugged them tight as I could. I wanted to cry, but I kept it together.

By the way, I never got my money back from the wedding trip.

Every Aruba trip he's went without me, he was fucking other bitches. Basically, a fucking spree!

After the divorce was final, I called Chris and he didn't answer. I text Chris to let him know, the divorce was final and I needed my settlement from when I put $15K down on the house. Chris sent the money back, but refused to send me the money for the down payment on the winery. He still had my club lights and my damn sex toys!

I never received the money from the winery and I called him to tell him about the toys and I was watching his ass. Chris interrupted me abruptly after mentioning the toys and yelled, "Is that's why you're calling me?" and he hung up in my face.

I called him back and he didn't answer, so I text Chris letting him know it would be his best interest to answer the phone, but I received a voicemail. Apparently, he butt-dialed me and he was talking about my ass, but when I heard a woman's voice saying, "OMG", I fucking lost it and went straight to Facebook Live blasting his ass! Since, he didn't want to hear me over the phone.

He quickly found out about the Live, because I addressed him and his bitch! Y'all, do you remember the woman who was at Chris's birthday/wine fest, who was looking and acting crazy with me? That was the Bitch! She was basically his date at his little birthday party!

Friends are not true friends, when they can't stand up to you and tell you, when you're wrong. All of his friends acted as if nothing was happening! I can't be that type of friend, nor a family member. My friends will get in my ass whenever I'm wrong and I'm the same way with them. The sad part is, Chris is talking about you behind your back and telling your business to anyone who will listen.

One day, on my way to Macon, Georgia to see my brother perform, one of the chicks from Huntsville sent me a friend request on Facebook. Now Chris told me in the past she was a cool person, but when she sent a request while we were together, he told me not to accept her.

"Did you fuck her or something? How come you don't want me to be friends with her?"

He told me no and the woman and her friends were messy. Chris also told me to stay away from them.

I went on accepted her friend request and told her to call me. Right off of the bat, she and Chris were sleeping together and he was also sleeping with her girlfriend too. He told her that we weren't together. On top of that, he pitted her against her friend to avoid letting them know, he was fucking them while being with me. Y'all, this is what really took me out, she told me he is bisexual as well!

"Damn! You know what? I can see this, because I have never seen a man acts the way he does as far as arguing and other petty shit!"

If this is true, he needs to live his truth and stop destroying people lives and I left it at that with her.

The Fourth Wife

In October during Magic City Classic Weekend, I was hosting an event at The Vault with all of the mayors in the State of Alabama. I was getting ready, when one of my friends called me wanting to talk.

She said, "Do you remember when I came by to the apartment to see you while I was in Huntsville?"

"Yes."

She continued, "When your husband came in, he spoke and went outside to smoke his cigar. "

"Yes, I remember that."

"After I left out the door, he was standing by her car and told me whenever you got off the with me, you would call another friend and talked about me.", she said.

What kind of man say some shit, like that?

"Why didn't you come back in the apartment and tell me what he said?"

She told me, she figured something was wrong with him and drove off.

"You are my best friend for over 35 years and I'm more hurt you didn't tell me, what he did."

"I kept telling y'all, Chris didn't want me around

anyone, but him."

She said, "I see what you were saying now!"

My Message

Nowadays, I take it day by day, because my heart is still broken and I feel so numb inside. I pray twice a day; sometimes more knowing God is here for me and he will get me through this. I will never hold another man accountable for what Chris has put me through, because I know, I want true love and I will have it one day.

I never thought in a million years, this would be my life right now. How did I let this happen to me? I loved Chris so much, I was willing to give up everything for him. He had my whole heart and broke me down to nothing. Even today, I still feel empty inside. I know in time; God will heal my heart.

In the end, I loved myself more and had to let him go. Pay attention to the signs and red flags! If it ever becomes physical, you need to get out! I want every man and woman to know, you're worthy of true love and we all deserve it. Don't settle and don't let anyone use you or abuse you. You are worthy of everything God has for you.

I am patiently waiting on my King, who is waiting for me and ultimately, TRUE LOVE.

Narcissistic Checklist

COMMON FEELINGS IN A NARCISSISTIC RELATIONSHIP

- Feeling "not good enough"
- Self-doubt and second-guessing
- Chronically apologetic
- Confusion and as though you are "losing your mind"
- Helplessness and hopelessness
- Sadness and depression
- Feeling anxious and worried
- Feeling unsettled
- Anhedonia
- Feelings of shame
- Mental and emotional exhaustion

Narcissist Check List

1. Two Faced, putting friends and family down behind their backs.
2. Tendency to blame their lack of success and failures on others.
3. Acts different in public than in private.
4. Irresponsible and unreliable
5. Arrogant, acts superior to people close to them.
6. Lives in a fantasy world which may include porn, flirting, affairs, and dreams of unlimited success and fame.
7. Addicted to this fantasy oriented behavior.
8. Will lie and distort facts and change events to suit their own agenda.
9. Be irresponsible with money
10. Emotionally distant and unavailable unless they want something.
11. Lack sympathy for others, especially those they exploit.
12. Be very controlling and unable to relax.
13. Regularly provoke people and blame them for the fight.
14. Have trouble admitting their mistakes.

Made in the USA
Middletown, DE
10 July 2020